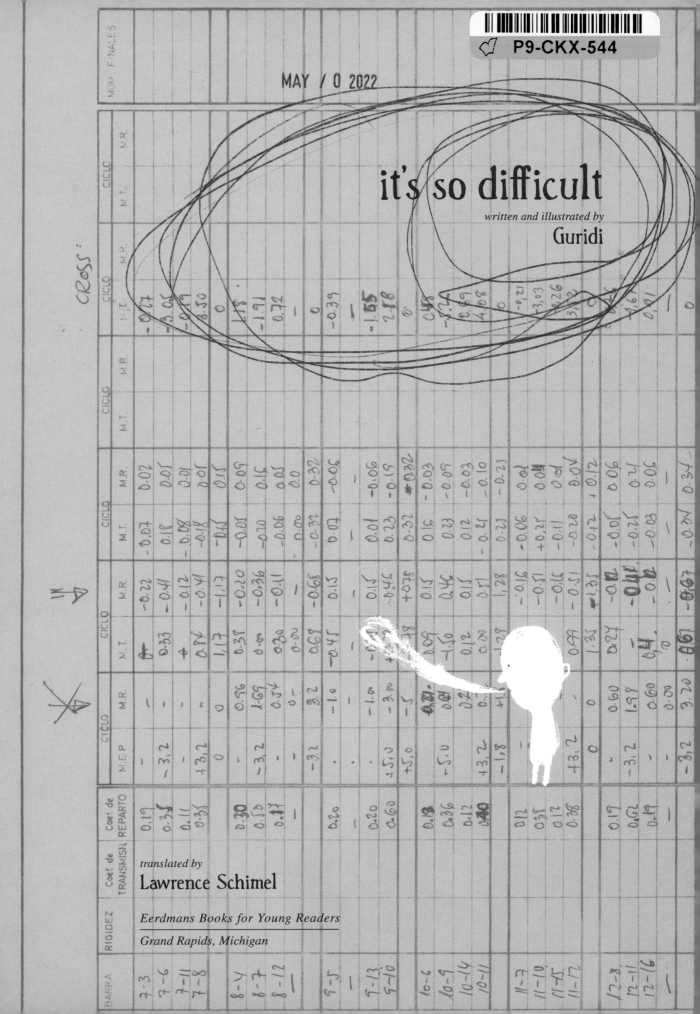

it's so difficult

written and illustrated by

Guridi

translated by

Lawrence Schimel

Eerdmans Books for Young Readers

Grand Rapids, Michigan

When I leave the house, everything is so difficult for me.
I feel a prickling that won't go away,
and every step I take is a triumph.

I'd like to say "hello" to the baker,
to my neighbor Ana,
to Miss Antonia.
And to say something like . . . "What a pretty dress
  you're wearing!"
But I only manage a smile . . .
I smile . . . just that.

It's so difficult to speak . . .

I count things until I reach the sign for the 21 bus stop.
There is a man there who breathes very loudly.
The bus took seventeen breaths to arrive—
I counted.

Counting things or calculating relaxes me.

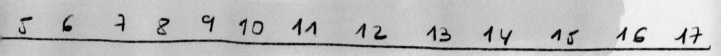

5   6   7   8   9   10   11   12   13   14   15   16   17

The bus driver still doesn't know what my voice sounds like.
I only stretch out my hand with the fare.
Just that.

He always asks me how I am,
without expecting an answer.
I wouldn't know what to tell him anyway.

It's such a difficult question to respond to . . .

I smile and quickly look for a place to sit.
I look at my shoes.
A man shouts. I don't like it when people shout.
I don't want to look at the person who sits down next to me.

I prefer to distract myself by looking at every shape,
every color of the city.
But what if people say something to me?

It's so difficult to concentrate . . .

Arriving at school is always complicated.
Greetings, laughter, fathers and mothers saying goodbye,
lots of people all talking at the same time.

Everyone is present in class.
Her, him, and him. And them, too.
I know each and every one of their names.
They don't know that I do, though,
because I've never said their names aloud.

It's so difficult to say their names . . .

My mother always tells me not to rush myself.
That someday the words will happen.

But it's just so difficult for them to come out . . .

In a quiet voice I can say little things,
but my heart beats very fast and I feel afraid.
In a quiet voice I've said things like:

                                "yes,"

                                        "fine,"

                                                "thanks."

They say that, with time, I'll get better.
That I need to be patient.
But I see older people who can't say what they feel
or what they think.
People who prefer not to speak
or smile.

It might be because of the noise.
The noise makes everything so difficult . . .

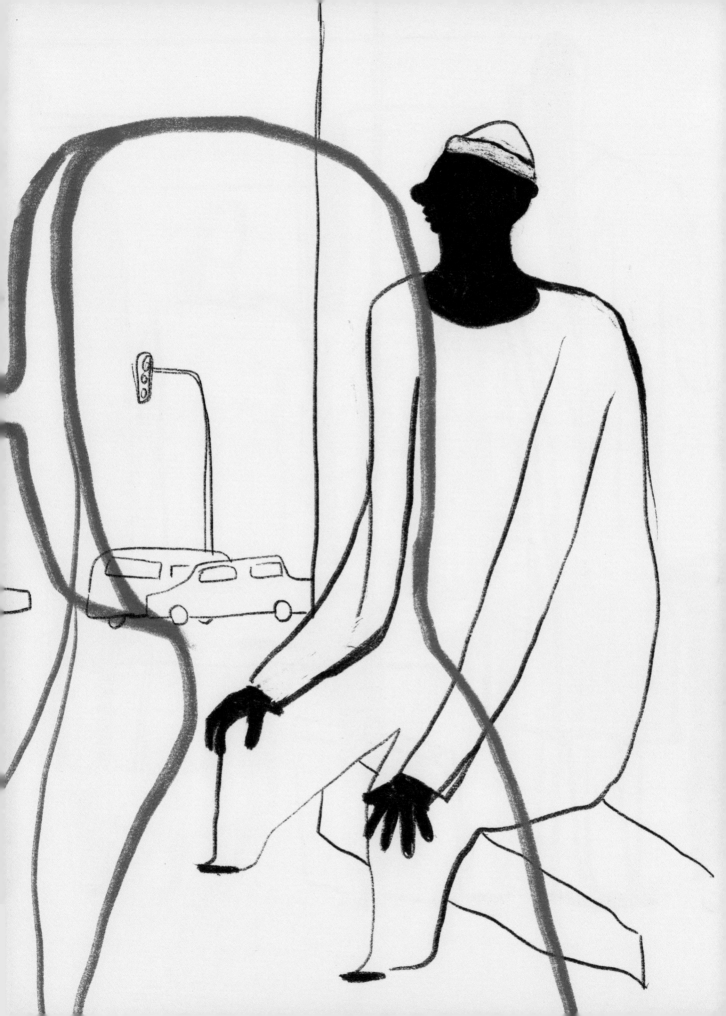

Right now, my hands are sweating.
It's hard for me to breathe.
But, this time, I'm going to manage to do it . . .

But . . .
It's just that . . .

It's so difficult . . .

CROSS:

A =

NUDO	BARRA	RIGIDEZ	Coef de TRANSMISN	Coef de REPARTO	CICLO M.E.P.	M.R.	M.T.	M.R.	CICLO M.T.	M.R.	CICLO M.P.	M.T.	M.R.	CICLO M.T.	M.R.	CICLO M.T.	M.R.
7	7-3			0.19	—	—	0	-0.22	-0.07	0.02			-0.27		
	7-6			0.35	-3,2	—	0.33	-0.4	0.18	0.05			-3.05		
	7-11			0.11	—	—	0	-0.12	-0.08	0.01			-0.19		
	7-8			0.35	+3,2	—	0.32	-0.4	-0.18	0.05			3.50		
	—			0.36	0	0	1,17	-1,17	-0,1	0,15			0		
8	8-4			0.30	—	0.96	0.38	-0.20	-0.05	0.05			1.15		
	8-7			0.53	-3,2	1.69	0.06	-0.36	-0.20	0.16			-1.91		
	8-12			0.17	—	0.55	0.30	-0.1	-0.06	0.05			0.72		
	—			—	—	0	0.02	—	0.0	0.0			—		
9	9-5			0.20	-3,2	3.2	0.45	-0.08	-0.32	-0.06			-0.39		
	—			—	—	-1.0	0.45	0.15	0.07	—			—		
	9-13			0.20	+5,0	-1.0	0.01	0.15	0.01	-0.06			-1.55		
	9-10			0.60	+5,0	-3,0	+0.32	-0.45	0.23	-0.19			2.18		
					+5,0	-5	-0.48	+0.48	-0.32	+0.28			0		
10	10-6			0.12	-5,0	0.21	0.09	0.15	0.16	-0.03			0.48		
	10-9			0.36	-5,0	0.61	-0.50	-0.45	0.23	-0.05			-5.25		
	10-14			0.12	—	0.21	0.12	0.15	0.12	-0.03			0.69		
	10-11			0.40	+3,2	0.72	0.99	0.11	-0.22	-0.10			4.08		
	—			—	-1,8	1.18	-1.28	1.28	-0.21	-0.23			0		
11	11-7			0.12	—	—	0.09	-0.16	-0.06	0.07			-0.21		
	11-10			0.35	-3,2	—	0.36	-0.51	+0.27	0.04			-3,03		
	11-15			0.12	—	—	—	-0.16	-0.11	0.07			-0.26		
	11-12			0.38	+3,2	—	0.99	-0.51	-0.20	0.0			3,52		
					0	0	1.35	-1,35	-0.12	+0.12			0		
12	12-8			0.17	—	0.60	0.24	-0.30	-0.05	0.05			0.74		
	12-11			0.62	-3,2	1.58	—	-0.51	-0.25	0.12			-1,67		
	12-16			0.19	—	0.60	—	-0.15	-0.03	0.05			0,91		
	—			—	—	0.0	—	—	-5,0				0		